For Debbie T.

Aladdin Books
Macmillan Publishing Company
866 Third Avenue, New York, NY 10022
Maxwell Macmillan Canada

First Aladdin Books edition 1994

Copyright © 1993 by Fiona Pragoff

First published in Great Britain 1993
by Victor Gollancz
A Cassell imprint
Villiers House, 41/47 Strand, London WC2N 5JE

1 2 3 4 5 6 7 8 9 10

ISBN 0-689-71814-4

Printed in Hong Kong

Fiona Pragoff

IT'S GREAT
TO BE TWO

ALADDIN BOOKS
Macmillan Publishing Company New York
Maxwell Macmillan Canada Toronto
Maxwell Macmillan International New York Oxford Singapore Sydney

When you are two
There's lots you can do.

You play with your shapes
And build with bricks.

Sometimes you're noisy.
You don't want to stay still.

You like your mealtimes

And reading your books

You can draw and paint

And take off your clothes

At bathtime.